For Mike – D.M.
For Alan, Harriet and Tom – A.S.

First published in the United States 1992
by Dial Books for Young Readers
A Division of Penguin Books USA Inc.
375 Hudson Street, New York, New York 10014

Published in Great Britain by
Frances Lincoln Limited

Library of Congress Cataloging in Publication Data
MacKinnon, Debbie.
What shape? / by Debbie MacKinnon;
photographs by Anthea Sieveking. — 1st ed.
p.   cm.
Summary: Brief text and photographs introduce a variety of shapes
as curious toddlers explore the world around them.
ISBN 0-8037-1244-8
1. Geometry—Juvenile literature. [1. Shape.] I. Sieveking, Anthea. ill. II. Title.
QA445.5.M33   1992   516'.15—dc20   91-34700   CIP   AC

WHAT SHAPE?

Debbie MacKinnon

Photographs by Anthea Sieveking

Dial Books for Young Readers New York

What shape is Claudia's tunnel?

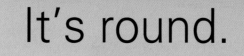

It's round.

more round things

teething ring

bowl

tomato

clock

balls

What shape is Oliver's sandbox?

It's square.

more squares

activity toy

dice

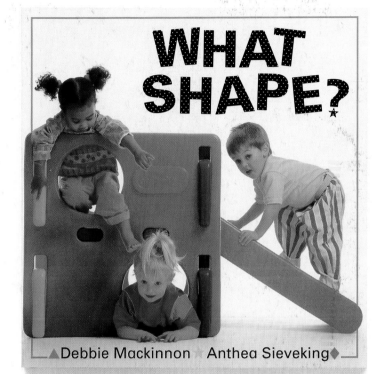

book

jigsaw puzzle

soft blocks

What shape is Gemma's tent?

It's a triangle.

more triangles

sandwiches

cheese

paper
napkin

cake

party hat

pizza

What shape
is Jack's
basket?

It's an
oval.

more ovals

chocolate
eggs

baby shoes

grapes

pebbles

pinecone

egg

sponge

What shape
is Andy's
balloon?

It's a
heart.

more hearts

picture
frame

box of
chocolates

soap

paint set

erasers

bracelet

What shape is Sabrina's wand?

It's a star.

more stars

cookies

stickers

cookie
cutter

starfish

baby
toy

sunglasses

What
shape
are Sam's
buttons?

They're
diamonds.

more diamonds

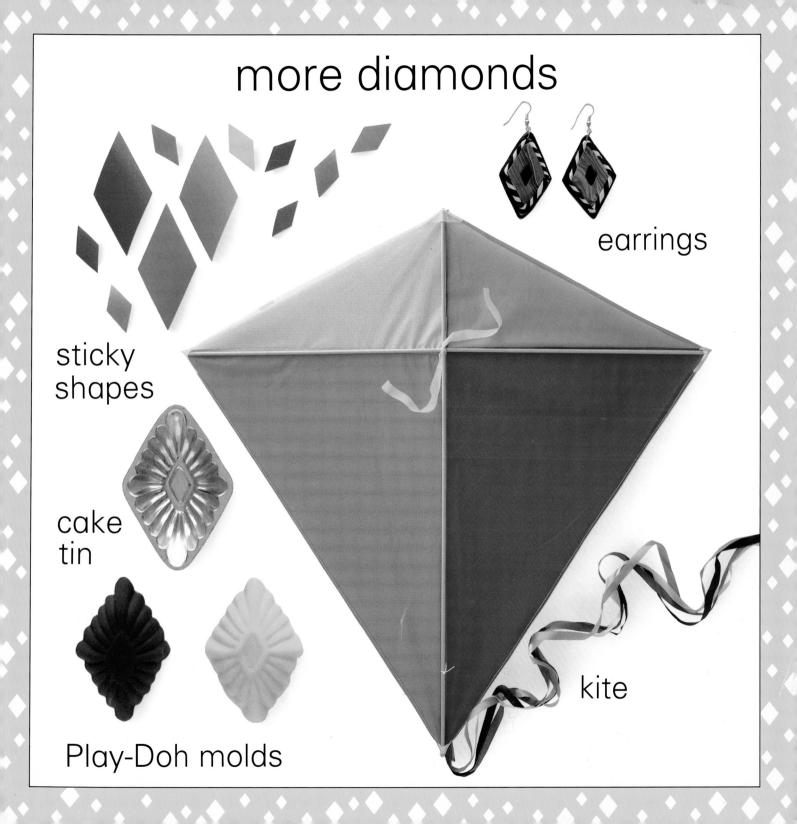

earrings

sticky shapes

cake tin

Play-Doh molds

kite